KT-225-273

RAVENS' REVENGE

Anthony Masters

Illustrated by Peter Dennis

A & C Black • London

CHAPTER ONE

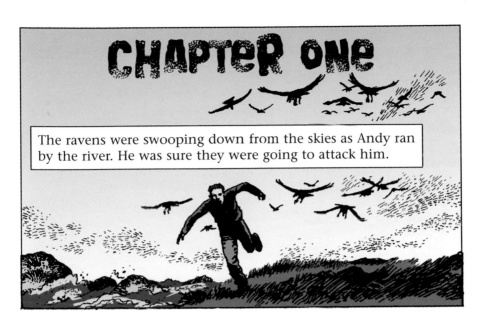

The ravens were swooping down from the skies as Andy ran by the river. He was sure they were going to attack him.

Suddenly, one of the beaks stabbed his forehead. Another ripped at his hair. Yet another grazed his cheek and he was soon smarting with pain, the blood running into his eyes.

Andy fell, knuckles bleeding, curling up into a ball against the vicious attack.

Andy!

For a few minutes there was silence. The sky was black with circling ravens. Then they swooped again, beaks slashing.

Slowly, he began to surface from the nightmare.

Andy! Wake up!

You're having a bad dream.

Somehow, he struggled to wake up and sat up in bed, sweating and trembling.

You were shouting.

Andy's mother looked down at her son in concern.

I wonder if you've got a touch of the flu.
Maybe you shouldn't go to Greystone after all.

No chance.

I've been looking forward to that
advanced course all year. There are prizes
to be won and I'm in the mood for winning!

Greystone Grange was a ruined Victorian mansion with a canoe centre in the outbuildings.

When Andy arrived by taxi from the station, he saw something in the blue July sky that gave him a nasty shock.

A raven was flying overhead in slow, graceful circles. Then it was joined by another.

Andy shivered, remembering his nightmare.

That night, lying in his bunk bed, Andy dreamt of ravens yet again. They were flying over his head, making their sad cawing sound as he paddled his canoe in the fast-running river that flowed past the ruins of Greystone Grange. He woke with a start.

Andy clambered out of his bunk. He had to take a shower. He had to get the ravens out of his head.

CHAPTER TWO

The current was fast and spray broke over the bow of Andy's canoe. Bill Ford, the course instructor, followed Andy.

But Andy felt as if he were part of the river itself.
It was an extraordinary feeling.

There was only one other student who seemed as confident as he was. Andy had noticed her right away.

There was something very positive about Kate.
Andy had noticed that when they first met.
Positive and challenging.

As they rounded a bend, Andy looked up into the sky.
With a sigh of relief, he saw there wasn't the slightest
sign of a raven. Why did the birds bother him so much?
Why had he dreamt about them?

Bill came alongside Andy and Kate in calmer water.

Then Andy noticed an older boy paddling expertly towards them, while the other two instructors were busy rescuing students who had capsized.

Jack smiled at Kate, ignoring Andy.
He had black hair and a beaky nose.

Andy felt threatened by this confident-looking boy who
seemed interested only in Kate.

Andy and Kate had to struggle to keep up.

Following Jack as best he could, Andy looked up at the sky. He saw a lone raven descending. The muscles in his arms felt as if they were going to burst as he ripped through the water with his paddle.

He could hear Kate gasping. Was she as exhausted as he was? Why didn't Jack slow down? Or was he just showing off?

Then, as they rounded another bend, Andy saw the rapids.

The current was now flowing much faster. Spray flew high into the air, falling on the jagged rocks that rose out of the river. Kate was alarmed.

Jack was smiling now.

Raven Rapids are really tough.

So are you, thought Andy.
You even look a little like a raven.

Andy's canoe was already bumping against the rocks and he
frantically tried to fend them off with his paddle. But as he got
the feel of the current, he grew more confident again.

Exhilaration filled Andy, and he turned to see Kate paddling behind him in a sheet of spray.

Andy's loss of concentration was fatal. As he swung back, he saw his canoe was being hurled towards a jagged rock.

Then he saw a raven sitting on top of the rock.

Andy heard the loud caw above the roaring of the rapids.
His canoe spun around and capsized.

Andy pushed down hard at the cockpit with his hands – and
came out of the canoe like a cork from a bottle.

As the current took him, the raven flapped its wings, soaring into the summer sky, cawing as if in triumph.

Held up by his life jacket, Andy bumped down to the bottom of the rapids. He stood up in the shallow water, gasping, bruised and shaken.

Andy's pride was hurt. Jack was grinning. Kate looked worried.

Andy looked back to see the small craft caught behind a rock and being pounded by the current.

Andy turned away and trudged up the path beside the rapids. He felt badly humiliated.

Eventually, he managed to grab his canoe and tow her down behind him. He slipped over several times and he could hear Jack laughing. Then he heard Kate laughing, too.

I hope you haven't damaged it.

I don't think so.

Andy looked up at the sky, which was clear and empty.
He felt his anger boiling.
They arrived back at the centre. Jack had a proposal.

Why don't you both have a shot at the Greystone Cup?

What's that?

Andy felt stupid for not knowing.

That's a real challenge. You have to shoot Raven Rapids without touching a single rock. That's how you win. No practising in advance, either. Raven Rapids are tough.

I'll have a go.

Kate was more enthusiastic.

I'd love to try. Do you think I'm good enough?

Of course you are.

CHAPTER THREE

That night, there was a campfire on the grass outside the ruined mansion.

All the members of the canoe course sat round a blazing fire, cooking and eating sausages and beefburgers.

Know any ghost stories?

There was a long silence. Then Jack spoke quietly.

I wouldn't say I've got a ghost story exactly.

Then what have you got?

Jack paused.

He was staring hard at Andy, the little smile back on his lips, and Andy felt a stab of fear.

Jack looked down into the flames.

The Grange has always been the family home of the Dentons. They've died out now. At least most of them have, and that's why the place is a ruin.

Jack looked back at the gaunt, crumbling chimneys.

Years ago, one of the younger sons fell in love with this girl. She was a stranger.

What was the guy's name?

Andy spoke without thinking. He didn't want Jack to know how much he was getting to him.

There was another long silence. Then someone called out, "Finish the story."

As I said, John fell in love with this stranger, but she didn't want him. So he went mad with grief and was just about to throw himself into the rapids when he saw a young raven with a broken leg. John put the bird's leg in a splint, and eventually the raven got better.

Is that all?

UXBRIDGE COLLEGE
LEARNING CEN

Jack grinned.

Andrew.

What a horrible story.

By the way...

Jack was still grinning.

I'm a distant cousin of the Dentons.

Andy was running beside the river and the ravens filled the sky above him, a hovering, dark mass. Then they rose higher and dived. Their eyes red with rage, their beaks sharp as needles.

Andy tried to beat them off, but he knew his efforts were hopeless.

Now they were tearing at his eyes and he began to scream.

Kate's voice was anxious.

Andy! Wake up.

He woke to see the dying flames, and Kate and Jack sitting together. All the others had gone to bed.

You were having a bad dream.

Kate sounded just like his mother had yesterday morning.

A very bad dream.

31

CHAPTER FOUR

When he woke the next morning, Andy heard shouting. Scrambling out of his bunk, he hurried outside to find Bill and Jack having a row. They were furious with each other.

Stop bothering Kate!

Bill lowered his voice as Andy came up.

She's fine.

Shut up!

Bill turned to Andy.

34

Kate and Andy were practising on the rapids they had shot the day before.

Then, as Andy dragged his canoe up the path for another try, he saw a single raven hovering overhead. He felt the fear pumping inside him, but he was determined not to let the bird put him off.

Reaching the top of the rapids, Andy launched his canoe.
He had to do well, he had to beat Kate.

As his canoe was caught up in the current, he began to swirl
past the rocks.

For a while he kept his cool, forcing himself not to look up,
not to watch the raven hovering above him.

Watch me!

But Andy could see the shadow of the bird on the prow of
his canoe.

When he glanced up, the raven was
only a few yards above his head.

Then the thing began to dive.

Suddenly his canoe was moving sideways, hitting
rocks as the fragile craft began to descend the
rapids, completely out of control.

The canoe flipped over and Andy was trapped upside
down. He beat with his fists at the side of the craft.

I'm gone if someone doesn't help me!

He'd never liked eskimo rolling and the current was incredibly
strong. But still no one came to his rescue and Andy was sure
he was going to drown.

Help!

Water filled his mouth and he choked and gasped, still beating frantically with his fists.

Then, suddenly, the canoe was dragged away by the current and Andy found himself floundering in shallow water.

Kate was on the bank, staring down, looking terrified. Jack was beside her, watching. Andy wondered where he had come from.

He looked up at the sky, searching for the raven.

Then Andy heard a low cawing and saw the bird sitting on the branch of a tree that overhung the river.

The raven's eyes were piercing and Andy thought they seemed triumphant.

When they got back for lunch, Kate pulled Andy to one side.

But Kate was hardly listening.

Kate didn't enjoy telling on Jack, but she patiently explained to Bill that Jack wouldn't leave her alone.

He was watching Jack effortlessly rolling his canoe on the river.

CHAPTER Five

Bill took them out on the rapids that afternoon and
Andy did much better. There was no sign of any ravens.
He paddled down the rapids twice without capsizing.
So did Kate.

Back in the calm of the shallows, Bill was impressed.

Well done. You both stand a chance of
winning the Cup. I think we should go for
the challenge tomorrow morning.

Then a dark cloud of ravens rose cawing from the ruins, soaring up towards the sun. Andy shivered and glanced at Kate. But she was looking away, staring down at the fast-flowing river.

The next day, Andy and Kate got up early to find Jack by the river. He looked upset.

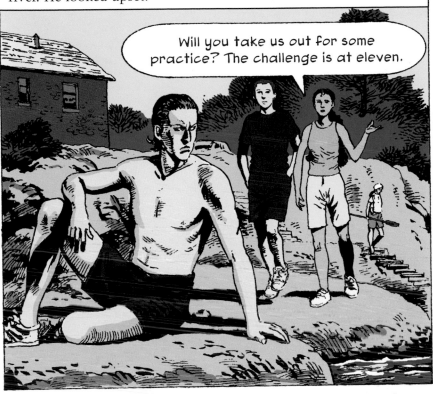

Jack grinned at her and Andy thought he looked more like a raven than ever.

Jack got to his feet, stretching lazily. He was wearing swimming shorts and the muscles in his arms bulged.

OK, OK. I'll take you both.

Why are you always so rude?

Oh, I'm sorry if I upset you.

Andy knew Jack wasn't sorry at all.

CHAPTER SIX

Andy stared down at the damage in disbelief. Somebody had attacked his canoe with an axe.

Jack was suddenly more helpful.

They looked up as a lone raven began to circle overhead.

They were standing overlooking Raven Rapids, which were much wilder than the smaller rapids downstream. The current had never looked so menacing. There was a strong wind and the torrent was breaking over the rocks, sending up a misty spray. Andy looked down at his brand-new canoe and sighed. He had no other choice. He'd have to give her a go.

Andy and Kate were sitting nervously in their canoes just above the rapids. The rest of the course had come to watch and there was a feeling of expectation. Kate's canoe was rocking gently.

A feeling of panic swept over Andy as he saw the ravens once again rising from the ruins. They seemed to be heading directly for him. Then he saw Jack. He was grinning again.

CHAPTER SEVEN

The water was coming over the bow of Andy's canoe in sheets, soaking him. Desperately steering his paddle at high speed, he found the current was pushing him through a narrow channel between the rocks.

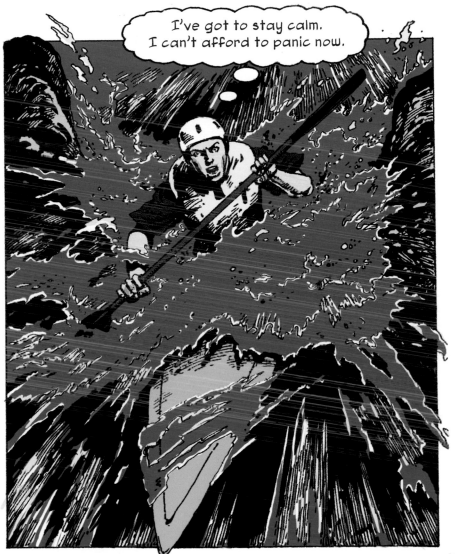

Andy's canoe took the tight bends with long, low, sweeping movements. Just like a bird, just like a raven. A rush of confidence filled him as he swooped and glided.

The crowd was running down the steep path that ran beside the rapids, cheering and shouting. There was no sign of Jack. Then Andy saw Jack was in his canoe below, with a raven hovering over his head.

Andy's fears abruptly returned and he almost capsized, his paddle flailing, suddenly out of control.

Desperately he tried to concentrate, and got some of his confidence back as he hurtled between the rocks. Somehow he avoided them all until, gasping and shaking, he met up with Jack in the calm pool below the rapids.

Soon Kate shot down to join them, raising her paddle in the air with a whoop of joy.

During the cheering, Andy glanced
at Jack. He was frowning.

CHAPTER EIGHT

Andy lay exhausted on his bunk. The celebration that evening had ended an hour ago, but despite the relief at having done so well, he couldn't sleep.

> Didn't you graze that big rock as you came down?

Jack's scornful voice repeated again and again in his head.

Then Andy heard a cawing sound and sat up in his bunk, cracking his head on the one above. Ravens didn't fly at night, did they? Shouldn't they all be in their roosts? Then he heard a light tapping sound.

Someone – or something – was knocking at the glass. Taking care not to wake the others, Andy tiptoed over to the window.

All he could see outside was a dark, fluttering shape.

Then Andy realised he was gazing into the eyes of a raven.

Black wings flapping, the bird flew down and landed on the grass. In the moonlight, Andy saw a figure walking towards the river. It was Jack. Andy crept across to the door and slipped outside.

Wait a minute! I want to talk to you.

The night was warm and muggy, and he thought he detected a growl of distant thunder. The raven stared up at him without the slightest sign of fear. It turned towards the figure on the lawn.

Jack's feet were bare and he looked as if he were sleepwalking. He was taking slow, deliberate steps and his arms were pressed to his sides.

But he didn't seem to hear. Andy began to walk quickly towards him. Jack was only a couple of metres from the river now and Andy could hear its muted roar.

Andy broke into a run.

Jack's eyes seemed hooded and the raven fluttered towards them.

Andy didn't want to fight.

Jack hit Andy again and this time Andy lost his temper.
He ran at Jack with his fists out. Then, as if in slow motion,
they toppled into the lashing, foaming river.

Andy gasped as the cold water took his breath away. The current
was strong and he felt weak and helpless in its grip.

He spluttered as he swallowed water, and then looked round for
Jack, who had just surfaced with a huge cut on his
forehead that was bleeding badly.

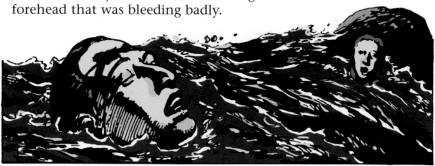

Andy tried to reach him, but the current was much stronger
now, taking both of them down towards Raven Rapids.

Andy looked up to see a great black cloud over the face of the moon. Then the cloud began to break up.

Sure enough, Andy could see them now, hundreds of birds diving down from the sky towards the rapids, coming straight at him.

Now they were both being whirled around in circles as the current swept them towards the bend of the river.

The ravens swooped lower. Was there something in the river they wanted, wondered Andy? Could that something be him?

The ravens and their snapping beaks were nearer now, just a few centimetres above Andy's head.

Andy gasped and choked as he swallowed more water.

Dimly, he heard the sound of someone shouting and saw Kate and Bill running along the bank towards them.

Kate's voice seemed to come from a very long way away.

But Jack didn't reply and when Andy searched for him in the moonlight, he could see he was floating on his back. Jack's eyes were open and the dark blood from the gash on his forehead was flowing even faster.

The rope landed in the river with a splash, but fell short.

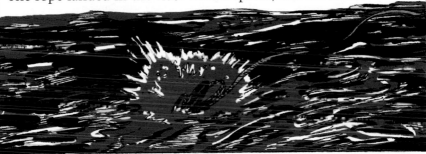

Andy glanced up at the ravens yet again. They had risen, grouping together, making a mass cawing sound.

Andy began to strike out hard, doing a fast crawl, swimming towards Jack, exerting as much strength as he could against the current. But they were still being swept around the bend and Andy knew the rapids weren't far ahead.

Then he saw a tree that had fallen over the bank. If only he could push Jack into its branches, then he might stand a chance of surviving. Andy knew he had to find more strength.

A raven skimmed the water, bathed in moonlight. Its beak was black and powerful. Its talons seemed to glow. In desperation, Andy struck out again, pushing Jack towards the tangle of dead branches. He managed to wedge him in the foliage and then clung on himself.

The river roared past, but he knew they were both safe now.

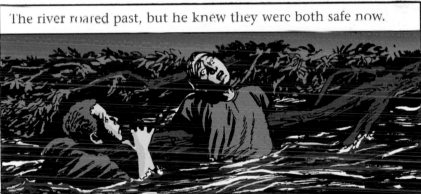

Andy watched the ravens flying up again towards the moon.

Bill scrambled over the dead tree. He grabbed Jack and pulled him gently towards the safety of the bank.

CHAPTER NINE

Then Bill managed to drag Andy back on land.
In a few minutes, Andy lay shivering next to Jack, who was
very still. One of the other instructors was kneeling beside him,
stopping the blood from the wound on his forehead.

Andy staggered to his feet.

Strong moonlight shone down on a young raven that was flopping around on the ground.

Jack opened his eyes slowly.

Bill gently picked up the raven, which struggled and then settled in his hand.

I'll fix the bird's leg and look after it until you're better. Trust me.

Jack nodded and closed his eyes again.

Bill turned to Andy.

What happened?

Jack was sleepwalking and heading towards the river. I tried to stop him, but we both went in.

Kate took Andy's arm and they both gazed up at the sky. The ravens were a hovering, dark mass. Then, slowly, they began to flutter down to the ruins of Greystone Grange.

But Andy wasn't so sure. He glanced up again. A single raven had started circling above him.